Magic Animal Friends

For Lily Grace Mutter

Special thanks to Valerie Wilding

ORCHARD BOOKS

First published in Great Britain in 2015 by The Watts Publishing Group

5 7 9 10 8 6

A CIP catalogue record for this book is available from the British Library.

ISBN 978 1 40834 847 5

Printed in Great Britain by Clays Ltd, Elcograf S.p.A

FSC www.fsc.org
MIX
Paper from responsible sources
FSC® C104740

The paper and board used in this book are made from wood from responsible sources

Orchard Books
An imprint of Hachette Children's Group
Part of The Watts Publishing Group Limited
Carmelite House, 50 Victoria Embankment, London EC4Y 0DZ

An Hachette UK Company
www.hachette.co.uk
www.hachettechildrens.co.uk

Emily Prickleback's Clever Idea

Daisy Meadows

ORCHARD

Shining House
Sunshine Meadow
Blossom Briar
Toadstool Cafe
Goldie's Grotto
Toadstool Glade
Mrs Taptree's Library
Library
Friendship Tree
Maze
Silver Spring
Buttercup Grove
Lighthouse

Map of Friendship Forest

Can you keep a secret? I thought you could!
Then I'll tell you about an enchanted wood.
It lies through the door in the old oak tree,
Let's go there now - just follow me!
We'll find adventure that never ends,
And meet the Magic Animal Friends!

Love

Goldie the Cat

Contents

CHAPTER ONE

Gold in the Mist

Lily Hart put the box she was carrying gently down on the grass. "This is the perfect place," she said, tucking her dark bobbed hair behind her ears.

Her best friend, Jess Forester, crouched beside her. It was an early Saturday morning, and the misty air was making her blonde hair even curlier than usual. "This is one of the best things about Helping Paw," she said. "Releasing animals back into the wild when they're better!"

Lily nodded. She felt so lucky that her parents ran the Helping Paw Wildlife Hospital in a barn at the end of their garden. She and Jess both adored animals and helped out there whenever they could. She carefully opened the box and smiled at the cute little hedgehog curled up inside. A man from Brightley Village had discovered it while he was walking

his dog. The hedgehog's leg had been hurt, so the man had taken it to Helping Paw. Now its leg was better, it was time for the hedgehog to be set free.

Lily imagined the little creature enjoying the smells of dewy grass and wet earth. "Time to go, little one," she said. Both girls watched in delight as the hedgehog waddled out. It snuffled as it explored the fallen leaves and twigs beneath the hedge.

As Jess watched, something else caught her eye…a flash of gold.

"Look, Lily!" she exclaimed. "Did you see that?"

"What?" asked Lily.

Jess peered through the mist. "I'm sure I saw golden fur," she said.

Lily felt a shiver of excitement. "Do you think it's Goldie?"

Goldie was a beautiful green-eyed cat, and the girls' special friend. She had taken them on lots of adventures in Friendship Forest, a magical world where the most amazing thing happened – all the animals talked!

"Yes, there she is!" cried Lily. Both girls ran to the tall clump of rushes that grew beside Brightley Stream. They stroked the golden cat while she purred happily, rubbing against their legs.

"I wish you could talk in our world, Goldie," said Lily. "Does Friendship Forest need help again, I wonder?"

A horrible witch called Grizelda wanted to drive the animals out of the forest so she could have it all to herself. Friendship Forest was full of beautiful trees and flowers, with the animals' gorgeous homes dotted among them. Grizelda wanted to turn it into a dark, gloomy place that only a witch would like. The girls and Goldie had managed to stop her evil plans so far, but now Grizelda had new magical helpers – dragons!

With a swish of her tail, Goldie bounded towards the stepping stones and crossed into Brightley Meadow.

Lily and Jess followed her towards the

lifeless oak tree that stood in the middle of the misty meadow. They knew what was going to happen next!

As Goldie reached the tree, it was suddenly bathed in sunlight. Leaves sprang from the branches and bright-yellow flowers blossomed in the grass below. Butterflies and bees appeared from nowhere and beautiful birdsong echoed all around.

"It's so exciting when the tree comes to life," Jess squealed, as letters appeared, carved into the broad trunk. Jess and Lily held hands and read them together. "Friendship Forest!"

As they spoke, a little door with a leaf-shaped handle appeared in the trunk.

Jess opened it and Goldie darted into the golden glow that shone inside.

The girls followed her through the door and into the shimmering light. They felt a tingly feeling all over. Lily squeezed Jess's arm happily, knowing that the tingle meant they were shrinking, just a little bit.

As the golden glow faded, the girls found themselves in a beautiful clearing surrounded by tall trees. Tiny cottages nestled among tree roots, and the warm air was filled with the scent of flowers. They were back in Friendship Forest! And in front of them, standing up with a golden scarf around her neck, was Goldie.

"Hello, girls," she said.

"At last we can talk to you!" cried Lily, as both girls hugged her.

"It's wonderful to be back in the forest," said Jess. "But is everything OK? Is Grizelda causing trouble?"

Goldie shook her head. "Everything is fine! I brought you here so I could take you to something special."

"Ooh, what?" asked Jess excitedly.

"The Rushy River Race!" Goldie cried.

CHAPTER TWO

The Waterwheel

"A boat race!" said Lily. "I can't wait!"

Goldie bent down to pick up a basket that was tucked in the roots of the Friendship Tree. "I've got another surprise for you!" she said with a smile. She opened the lid and the girls peeked inside.

"Mmmm! Blossom buns and watercress

sandwiches!" said Lily.

"Cherry bread!" said Jess. "And bottles of strawberry fizz – yum!"

"Everyone who goes to the Rushy River Race takes a picnic to share with their friends," Goldie said, shutting the lid.

Lily and Jess grinned at each other. Going to Friendship Forest was always exciting, but coming for a race and a picnic sounded even better!

"The race is at Willowtree River." Goldie continued as they walked. "Do you remember our adventure there?"

"Yes, that was when we rescued little

Ellie Featherbill," said Lily, smiling at the thought of the adorable duckling. Maybe they'd see her again today!

As they wandered through Toadstool Glade, Molly Twinkletail the mouse waved to them from the Toadstool Café. "Coo-ee!" she called from the window. The little mouse was sitting inside eating toffee toast with her mole friend, Lola Velvetnose.

"Hello, Molly!" said Jess and Lily.

Lola's little pink nose went *woffle woffle* as she sniffed to discover who Molly was talking to. "I smell honey," she said, peering through her round purple-framed glasses. "It's Jess!"

Lily laughed. "Lola always says you smell of honey, Jess," she said.

Lola's nose went *woffle woffle* again. "And that must be you, Lily," she said. "You smell of strawberries."

"Thank you, Lola!"

laughed Lily. "Are you coming to the Rushy River Race?"

"As soon as we've finished our toffee toast," said Molly. "I'm so excited!"

Jess, Lily and Goldie set off again, passing other animals on their way to the river. Some carried picnic baskets, some had rugs or sunshades, and everyone was chattering happily.

"What a beautiful day!" said Lily.

"The Shining House makes sure it's always sunny and warm here," remembered Jess happily.

"Thanks to you two," added Goldie.

The Shining House was cared for by the Flufftail squrriel family, who kept its magic working so that warm, bright sunlight always shone beneath the trees.

But recently Chilly, Grizelda's ice dragon, had put a spell on the poor squirrels and the magic had stopped until Jess and Lily had found a way to get the blue dragon to reverse his spell.

Goldie pointed through a gap in the trees. "There's Willowtree River!"

So many were animals crowded at the riverside that the girls could only just see the water, twinkling like a jewel in the sunshine.

"Look!" Goldie pointed her paw. The teams were getting ready by the starting line. The Featherbill duck family chatted beside their pretty blue and yellow barge. The Greenhop frog family had brought their widest lily pad, which was the size of Jess's kitchen table at home, and the Flippershell turtles were lining up too,

each wearing a cap of a different colour of the rainbow. Even their rowboat was rainbow-coloured, too!

Jess waved to the Paddlefoot beaver family, who were sitting one behind the other in their orange canoe. On the banks all around, animals were laying out their picnics and sat at a judge's table there were three elegant swan sisters. Silvia Whitewing, the eldest, nodded gracefully to the girls when they waved.

Then Goldie turned to the girls. "There's one more thing to do before the race can begin. Come on!"

Jess and Lily followed her downstream along the riverbank to a beautifully polished waterwheel. It turned slowly and steadily as its blades paddled through the water, making a lovely *splish splish* sound.

In front of the waterwheel, a family of hedgehogs were rolling around on the leaves and flowers that littered the riverbank. They spiked the leaves with their prickles, then scurried to shake them off onto a pile, well away from the waterwheel.

One of the smaller hedgehogs scurried over towards the girls.

"It's Harry Prickleback!" said Lily.

"Hello, Jess and Lily," said Harry, as two more adorable little hedgehogs looked curiously at the girls. "This is my brother Herbie. And this is our little sister, Emily."

Emily was wearing a pretty, sparkly tiara on her head. Lots of leaves and candyfloss-scented petals were caught in her prickles. "Excuse me," she said, touching Jess's knee. "I like your curly yellow hair."

"Thanks," said Jess. "I like your tiara!"

"Emily won that in a competition," Harry explained proudly. "She had to solve lots of really difficult puzzles."

Lily smiled at Emily. "You must be very clever," she said.

"Oh yes," said Mr Prickleback proudly. "Our little Emily is really smart!"

Emily's nose blushed pink.

"Your tiara looks so pretty with the

petals on your prickles," said Lily. "We should decorate our hair like that!"

Emily giggled. "It's not decoration," she explained. "It's work. We collect leaves and petals on our prickles so they don't clog up the waterwheel."

Mrs Prickleback bustled over to help get the leaves off Emily's back. "The Willowtree River flows when we turn the waterwheel," she explained. "We have to make sure it never stops, or the river will disappear."

"Only the Pricklebacks know how to turn the wheel," Goldie said. "That's why

I've come to ask them a favour."

Mr Prickleback grinned. "Anything for you, Goldie," he said.

"Will you make the river flow a little more quickly, please?" she asked. "We want to give the boats a flying start!"

The younger hedgehogs squealed in delight.

"Of course," said their dad. "Everyone, take your places!"

Lily and Jess grinned at each other happily. They couldn't wait to see the Pricklebacks in action!

CHAPTER THREE

Unwelcome Visitors

Jess and Lily watched the hedgehogs waddle over to the waterwheel. Inside it were five smaller wheels. Each of the Pricklebacks climbed into one.

"Ready, team?" asked Mr Prickleback.

"Ready!" they cried.

"Then one… and two… and…

Ready! Steady! CURL!"

The five hedgehogs immediately curled up into spiky balls. They rolled forwards, each making their own wheel turn. The five little wheels each turned a cog which clicked and clanked, then fitted together to turn the waterwheel. Suddenly the water started to rush through it much faster than before.

"Wow!" said Lily, as the hedgehogs rolled so quickly they became prickly blurs. "No wonder only the Pricklebacks can make the waterwheel work!"

But as the girls watched the waterwheel in delight, Goldie gave a cry. "Oh no!

Girls, look!" she shouted.

A familiar orb of yellow-green light was drifting through the trees, right towards them.

"It's Grizelda!" Jess called to the hedgehogs.

Emily stopped rolling and uncurled. Her little paws flew to her mouth. "The witch!" she squealed.

All the Pricklebacks stopped rolling. They jumped down from the waterwheel and huddled together, their spikes quivering with worry.

The orb burst in a shower of spitting

yellow-green sparks. In its place stood a

tall, bony woman with green hair swirling around her face like a bunch of snakes. She folded her arms and tapped the sharply pointed toe of one of her high-heeled boots.

"CURL!" Mrs Prickleback shouted. In a flash, all the hedgehogs rolled themselves into round, prickly balls.

"Your spiky little friends are right to be afraid," Grizelda sneered. "My next dragon is going to make all the animals leave this forest. Then it will be mine forever! Ha ha haa!"

Jess glanced at Lily. Her friend's eyes were wide, but she could tell Lily was determined not to let the witch see that she was scared.

"We're ready for anything your dragon does!" Jess said bravely.

"We'll see about that!" screeched Grizelda. Then, with a snap of her fingers, she disappeared.

Goldie slipped her paws into Jess and Lily's hands. "What do you think this dragon will do?" she asked.

They stood, backs together, watching and waiting. But the forest looked just as lovely as before.

The Pricklebacks had just started to uncurl when there was a mighty roar from above.

"Raaargh!"

Circling in the air was Dusty, Grizelda's yellow dragon!

The Pricklebacks seemed to be too frightened to move as the dragon gave a rasping giggle. "Heeheeheeheehee! I'm going to make it lovely and dry," she said. "Friendship Forest will be like a desert!"

Jess was horrified. "You can't do that!" she yelled. "What about the animals?"

"Heeheehee! Who cares about them?" said Dusty. "My yellow scales will look so pretty in the sun!"

Suddenly, she swooped lower.

"Oh no," cried Jess, "she's heading for the Pricklebacks!"

"Run!" shouted Lily.

"Hide!" yelled Goldie and Jess together.

But the Pricklebacks didn't move. They shook with fright, their spikes quivering.

Dusty flew towards them. She gave another sandy roar and chanted:

"Magic make these hedgehogs change
So they all turn to stone.
Then the river will flow no more,
But be as dry as bone."

Lily, Jess and Goldie watched in horror as the hedgehogs' brown prickles turned grey. Lastly their trembling paws turned grey and were still.

Jess ran to pick Harry up. His spikes were cold and as hard and he didn't feel like a real hedgehog at all. She clutched him to her and turned to Lily and Goldie. Her face was pale.

"Oh no!" she gasped. "The poor Pricklebacks. Grizelda's dragon has turned them to stone!"

CHAPTER FOUR

A Threat to Willowtree River

With a grinding noise, the waterwheel slowed to a stop.

The yellow dragon flew away, giggling to herself. "Heeheehee! Now the forest will be dry and lovely, just right for sunbathing!"

Goldie and Lily rushed over to the stone hedgehogs.

"Maybe they just need waking up," Lily said desperately.

Jess looked at Herbie. His black, beady eyes were open wide, and his little nose was frozen in the air. "Herbie?" she called, but the hedgehog didn't move.

"It's no good," Goldie said finally. "We can't break dragon magic, remember? Dragons have to reverse their spells themselves."

Jess was near to tears. "But we can't leave them like this," she said, "just four

tiny hedgehog statues."

Lily gasped. "Four!" she repeated. "There are only four of them."

Goldie grasped Lily's hands. "You're right!" she said.

Jess was puzzled. "What do you mean?" Then she realised. "Of course – there should be five! Where is little Emily Prickleback?"

As they stared around, they heard a faint squeak, then a little pile of leaves and petals started to uncurl, and a tiny, snuffly face peeked out.

"Emily!" cried Lily. "You had so many petals stuck on your prickles that Dusty didn't spot you."

She picked up the trembling creature, who snuggled into the crook of her elbow.

"What about my family?" Emily asked tearfully.

Jess stroked her cheek with a finger. "Don't you worry," she said softly. "We worked out how to get Chilly the ice dragon to reverse his magic. We'll find out how to make Dusty stop hers, too." Emily blinked back tears and clenched her little paws. "Mum and Dad say I'm good at working things out," she said, "so I'll help!"

Sadly leaving the statues behind, they hurried back up the river, where they found the animals clustered near the starting line, still waiting for the river to speed up so the race could begin. The Featherbill family were had started a water balloon fight and the ducklings were all waddling around, chasing each other with colourful water balloons. Ellie Featherbill squealed in delight as a balloon burst all over her fluffy feathers.

"Look," Mrs Featherbill cried. "The girls and Goldie are back!

Goldie quickly explained what had happened. Everyone started chattering with worry.

Agatha Glitterwing the magpie put a comforting wing around Emily. "We can't have the race now," she said. "Not while the poor Pricklebacks are under a spell!"

Lily was staring at the river. Something about it didn't look the same. "Does the river look shallower to you?" she asked Jess anxiously.

Emily raced to the riverside. "The

waterwheel must be stopping. The river's not just slowing down, it's disappearing!"

Goldie's whiskers quivered with worry. "We need to save Emily's family so they can get it turning again. If we don't, the river will turn as dry as bone, just like Dusty said in her spell!"

The Greenhops hopped up and down in a panic, croaking, "No Willowtree River? What will we do?"

"Oh my!" squawked Agatha. "All the trees and flowers will die, and we'll have nothing to drink!"

"We'll have to leave Friendship Forest!"

cried Mr Silverback the badger.

"That's exactly what Grizelda wants." Jess said. "Did anyone notice which way Dusty went?"

"She was going to sunbathe," said little Emily. "Maybe she's gone to the beach?"

Lily smiled at the hedgehog. "Brilliant idea, Emily! Your brothers were right – you really are clever."

Emily's nose went pink again.

"Coral Cove is close to here, " said Goldie. "It's a little sandy beach where Willowtree River turns a corner. We just need to follow the river. Come on, let's see

if Dusty's there!"

Emily rode in Jess's pocket, being careful not to prick her with her spikes, as the three friends set off.

"Good luck!" cried the Twinkletails.

"Take care," called Mr Silverback.

"Don't worry!" Goldie shouted back. "We'll save the Pricklebacks!"

Jess nodded. "After all, we've got a very clever hedgehog to help us..."

CHAPTER FIVE

Kingfishers in Trouble

The group of friends hurried past trees and bushes. Emily peeked out of Jess's pocket, holding her tiara in place with one paw.

Soon the bushes got so thick that they couldn't see the river at all. As they walked along, they heard a funny noise.

"Chee-kee, chee-kee!"

"It must be a bird." Lily said, thinking about the birds they sometimes helped at the Wildlife Hospital. "It sounds upset."

They pushed through the thick bushes to the river. As they got closer, they heard more and more bird voices crying out. "Chee-kee! Chee-kee!" they squawked.

When they reached the river, everyone gasped. The water had almost completely

disappeared, leaving only a muddy ditch behind. And stuck in the mud were five small birds! Their feathers were plastered with mud, leaves and bits of twigs.

"It's the Blueflash kingfisher family," Goldie cried, running to them. "Whatever has happened?"

"Chee-kee! Chee-kee!" Mrs Blueflash cheeped, ruffling her feathers with worry. "Oh, Goldie! We stopped for a dip on our

way to the Rushy River Race, so our colours would look fresh and bright. But now our wings are covered in thick mud so we can't fly!"

One of the little Blueflashes flapped his wings, but he couldn't take off. "We'll never get home again," he said sadly. "It's too far to hop."

"Don't worry, we'll help you," said Lily. "There must be a way we can clean your feathers."

"Lily and Jess help any animals in need," Goldie said comfortingly.

"But how?" Lily whispered anxiously.

"There's no water to wash them."

"Oh!" squeaked Emily. "I know how – I've had an idea!" She wriggled out of Jess's pocket and hopped down onto the ground. "Come here," Emily called to the Blueflash family. One by one the kingfishers hopped out of the ditch, looking bedraggled and sorry for themselves.

"Just copy me!" Emily showed them how to roll around on the ground just like hedgehogs. "The mud on your feathers has dried in the sunshine," she explained, "so if you roll, it will rub off!"

"It's a dust bath!" Jess giggled in delight.

The Blueflashes did as she said, and once they saw that Emily's plan was working, they all cheered up.

The young Blueflashes giggled as they rolled. Soon their brilliant blue and orange feathers were clean. They fluffed them up, then the kingfishers flapped their wings and took off, whizzing back and forth in delight.

"They're so fast that all I can see are blue flashes!" laughed Lily.

"Well done, Emily!" said Jess. "That was really clever."

Goldie told Mr and Mrs Blueflash about the spell Dusty had put on the rest of the Prickleback family.

"The beach is still quite far away," Mrs Blueflash told them. "But we'll see if she's there. We can be there and back in a flash."

"Thank you!" Jess called. The kingfisher family took off in a blur of colour. Minutes later they were back, shaking their heads. "She's not there." Mrs Blueflash told them.

"We'll keep an eye out for her," promised Mr Blueflash. "We really need the river back."

One of the youngsters fluttered past

them. "I'm cold," he said. "Let's fly up higher where the air is warmer!"

"Wait a minute! Could that be where Dusty is?" Lily wondered out loud. "She's not at the beach, but could she be sunbathing high among the treetops?"

Jess nodded. "It's worth a try."

Goldie's whiskers twitched. "But there are so many trees," she pointed out. "How do we know where she'd be?"

"Oh, I know!" said Emily. "She'd be up the tallest tree in the forest. That's the Treasure Tree!"

"Of course!" said Jess, remembering

that they'd climbed the tree on one of their adventures. "Your family are lucky you're so clever, Emily. We'll soon track Dusty down. Let's go!"

CHAPTER SIX

A Cleverfeather Invention!

The Treasure Tree towered above them, its leaves shimmering in the sunlight. There were all sorts of colourful fruits and nuts growing along its branches. Normally it was busy with animals gathering food, but today everyone was at the river and the Treasure Tree was deserted.

Jess peered into the branches. Was Dusty up there somewhere, sunning herself on the topmost branch? Magical vines hung around the trunk to help animals climb the tree safely. Jess ran to grab one, but nearly fell when she stubbed her foot on something hard.

It was a grapefruit, but it was made of stone!

"Dusty must have done this!" she cried, showing the others. "She's definitely here!"

"Goodness," said a voice nearby. "A pone stair – I mean a stone pear! This isn't right. Not right at all!"

Jess grinned. She knew that voice. It was Mr Cleverfeather the owl. Sure enough, when they looked behind the broad tree trunk, there he was with one of his inventions.

"Goldie!" he cried. "And Less and Jilly – I mean, Jess and Lily. Oh dear, I do get my words muddled. Are you picking fruit?

Would you like to borrow my invention? It's a ticking pool."

"A ticking pool?" said Emily, peeping out from Jess's pocket.

"He means a picking tool," Lily giggled. She jumped back as a stone coconut hit the ground with a thump.

Jess told Mr Cleverfeather about Dusty. "So you see," she finished, "we must get her to take the spell off the other Pricklebacks. If we don't, Willowtree River will be gone forever."

"There!" whispered Lily excitedly. "To the left of those bananas, above the coconuts. It's Dusty's tail!"

Sure enough, there was a yellow tail swinging lazily back and forth.

"Watch out!" cried Emily. "Pineapple!"

They leapt aside as a stone pineapple smashed through the branches, hitting the ground with a thud and shattering into tiny pieces.

There was a giggle from above. "Heeheehee!"

"Dusty must think it's funny to turn fruit to stone while she sunbathes," Jess said angrily.

"Look out!" said Goldie, dodging as a

stone walnut fell from the tree.

"Now we've dotted Spusty – I mean, spotted Dusty," said Mr Cleverfeather, "we must think of a way to get her down."

"If we can't," Emily said anxiously, "we'll never get her to reverse that spell."

They all thought hard.

"If only Dusty knew how much fun

water could be," Lily said, thinking about the Rushy Race and the lovely day they had planned.

Emily looked thoughtful. "It's like a puzzle," she said. "There must be something we can do..." Suddenly, she gave an excited squeak. "I know! Do you remember what the Featherbills were doing while everyone was waiting for the race to start?"

A grin spread over Jess's face as she realised what Emily meant. "They were having a water balloon fight!" she said.

"Emily, that's so clever!" said Lily. "Everyone loves water balloon fights."

"Even dragons?" Jess asked.

"Let's hope so," Goldie said, crossing her paws tightly.

Every inch of Mr Cleverfeather's inventing shed was crammed with tools and gadgets. Lily, Jess, Goldie and Emily peered around curiously. Jess grinned as she looked at the plans for a Cake

Creator which were spread out on the wise old owl's desk.

"My next invention," said Mr Cleverfeather, sweeping the plans aside. "But that's not what knee weed. I mean, we need." He rummaged around. "Banana-peeler for the parrots… no. Automatic ear-wash for rabbits… no. Ah!" he cried. "Here we are." He opened a large box.

Jess and Lily peered into it. "Water balloons!" they cried.

Mr Cleverfeather chuckled. "Ah, these aren't ordinary balloons," he said.

"They're Hi-Soak Balloons, just like the ones the Featherbills were using. I invented them so we could all have water fights on hot days. Great fun!"

"Perfect," said Goldie. "Hopefully Dusty will think it's fun too."

Mr Cleverfeather passed Jess a full watering can. Lily held a red balloon steady while Jess filled it. Then she knotted it and batted it into the air with her hand.

"Catch, Emily!" she said.

The little hedgehog tried to catch it, but she missed, and it landed on her prickly head and burst.

Pop!

It showered her with water.

Splosh!

Emily fell backwards in surprise, giggling so much that her tiara fell off.

Jess helped Emily to her feet. "But how will we fill up the balloons?" she wondered. "The river's gone."

"There's just enough water in the watering can to fill these ones," said Lily.

"And if our plan works, we'll get the

river back soon!"

While Mr Cleverfeather, Jess and Goldie filled as many balloons as they could, Lily used her skirt to pat Emily dry, then popped her back in Jess's pocket.

"Just one more thing," said Lily, "how can we throw them at Dusty? She's much too high up."

"Don't worry," said Goldie. "I'm sure our bird friends will help us make a very soggy delivery – of Hi-Soak Balloons!"

CHAPTER SEVEN

Attack!

Captain Ace flew above the treetops, towing his beautiful patchwork hot air balloon through the sky behind him.

Lily, Jess and Goldie were inside the basket hanging beneath the balloon, with a huge pile of filled water balloons at their feet. Emily perched on the side of the

basket, with Lily's

arm around her to

stop her falling off.

Captain Ace

pulled on a rope.

Puff! Puff! Puff!

Bubbles streamed up

into the balloon. Then they burst,

filling it with hot air.

Lily looked to the left and waved to

Mrs Taptree the woodpecker and her

chicks, Dig and Tipper, who

were flying alongside.

They gave muffled chirps. "Quick! Quick!"

Jess waved to the Blueflash family, who called, "Chee-kee! Chee-kee!" Their voices were muffled, too, because each bird had a bunch of water balloons dangling from its beak. Even tiny Jenny Littlefeather the wren was carrying one. Her wings beat twice as fast as the other birds' as she struggled to keep up.

Lily tightened her arm around Emily, and said to Jess, "Aren't we lucky to have so many wonderful friends?"

Jess nodded happily. "Look!" she cried, as they drew near to the Treasure Tree. "There's Dusty!"

The dragon was lying on her back on the topmost branch, her eyes closed and her wings outspread.

"Captain Ace," whispered Goldie, "can

we go a bit closer?"

The stork nodded.

They drifted along in silence. The birds flew as quietly as they could and Lily and Jess held their breath. If Dusty saw them before they could convince her to play, she could turn them to stone too, and they'd drop out of the sky!

Suddenly, the shadow of the hot air balloon fell on the dragon... and she opened her eyes.

"Oh no," gasped Jess. "She's seen us!"

Scrambling to her feet, Dusty let out a huge roar. "Raaargh!"

"Look out, Ace!" yelled Lily.

Ace flapped his wings hard, yanking the hot air balloon away from Dusty's roar. Lily and Jess could feel the blast of her hot breath, just missing the basket. The balloon rocked from side to side, sending the girls and Goldie toppling backwards in the basket.

"Hold on, Emily!" yelled Lily.

The little hedgehog was clinging onto the edge. But as the basket swayed, her paws slipped – and she fell over the side!

"Emily!" Lily cried.

Lily and Jess leaned out, expecting to

see the little hedgehog crashing through the branches below.

Instead, a terrified little face looked up at them from the edge of the basket. Two paws clung tightly on to a knotted rope.

Jess leaned over and scooped Emily up. "You're safe now," she said, cuddling her closely. Emily's prickles were standing on end with fright, but Jess didn't mind being spiked. "Are you all right, Emily?"

"I'm OK," Emily said, shakily.

The balloon drifted back towards the dragon, just out of reach of her hot sandy breath.

"Dusty!" called Goldie. "We've come to ask you something—"

"Pah!" interrupted the dragon. "Go away! Can't you see I'm busy sunning my pretty scales?" She lay down to sunbathe again.

"I think it's time to try our plan," whispered Lily. She called, "Dusty! Do you want to find out how much fun water can be?"

Dusty gave a growl. "Getting wet is NOT fun! My scales are only pretty when they're shining in the sun!" she snarled angrily. She beat her wings and took off, flying towards them, her mouth open.

"She's going to get us!" yelled Jess. "Quick, everyone… Fire!"

Lily and Jess grabbed balloons in both hands and threw them at the dragon. *Splat! Splosh!*

"Raaaaargh!" roared Dusty, flapping

around as the water drenched her yellow scales. "Raaaargh! I'm all wet!"

"Join in, Dusty!" Jess called, ducking as a water balloon sped over her head. "Missed me!" she laughed.

The birds carefully swooped down and put a pile of water bombs next to Dusty.

Dusty picked up a wobbly water balloon in her claws. Lily and Jess held their breath. Had it worked, or had they made the yellow dragon even angrier?

Splosh! Splat! Splosh! Water balloons were flying everywhere.

One of the balloons burst over Dusty's head. Without thinking the dragon threw the balloon at one of the woodpecker chicks, who burst out laughing as the water hit his feathers.

"Raaaa...heeheehee!" Dusty said, her roar becoming a giggle. Her scaly yellow face was surprised. "That feels funny!"

"It's working!" cried Goldie. "Dusty! Are you having fun?"

"Heeheehee!" chuckled the dragon, throwing a balloon at Goldie. Goldie giggled as it burst on her tail.

Dusty flew up into the sky, dodging and diving and throwing water balloons everywhere. Finally the dripping dragon landed back on the highest branch of the Treasure Tree. "More! More!" she cried.

Lily looked around. But everyone had used up all their balloons.

"We've run out of balloons, Dusty," Lily called. "And we can't fill up any more, because the river is all dried up."

Dusty looked upset. "But I want to carry on playing," she grumbled, her tail drooping.

"So do we," Jess told her. "But we need the river back first. Will you lift your spell

from the Pricklebacks so they can make it flow again?"

Dusty flew around in a loop-the-loop. "Yes," she agreed, "I will! Then we can play again!"

There was a chorus of happy cheeps, chirps and squawks from the birds. Captain Ace did a loop-the-loop, and the girls, Emily and Goldie gave a great cheer.

"Hooray!" cried Emily, her eyes shining. "We did it!"

CHAPTER EIGHT

The Rushy River Race

Captain Ace towed his hot air balloon, with its happy passengers, back to the waterwheel. Dusty flew beside them, giggling as water droplets shimmered on her scales. "My scales look even prettier," she boasted. "The water makes them sparkle even more than the sunshine!"

The balloon drifted over the muddy ditch where river should have been.

Captain Ace looked back. "Prepare for landing," he mumbled, with the rope still in his beak.

A few moments later, they were down. The birds landed next to the waterwheel and the girls, Goldie and Emily climbed out of the basket. Dusty skidded to a stop beside them.

Emily ran to her family and hugged the cold little stone figures. "You'll be back to normal soon," she said. "I promise!"

"Dusty's going to reverse the spell now," said Goldie. "Stand back, Emily!"

Dusty stood in front of the stone hedgehogs and chanted:

"Dragon wings stop Dusty's spell
Getting wet is great.
Make hedgehogs be themselves again,
And put the river straight."

The Pricklebacks started to turn from grey into their usual colours. They looked around in surprise.

Harry rubbed dust from his eyes. "What a weird dream I had," he said.

"Me, too," said Herbie.

"The dragon!" shouted Mrs Prickleback when she saw Dusty. "Where's Emily?"

"I'm here!" Emily cried, as Jess set her

down. She ran to hug and kiss her family. "You were made of stone!" Emily said, and she told her family everything that had happened.

"We couldn't have saved you without Emily," added Jess. "She's so clever!"

Emily's nose went extra pink as her family hugged her again.

Mr Prickleback gave a gasp. He pointed at the muddy ditch where Willowtree River was supposed to be flowing. "Oh my prickles!" he cried. "The river has gone!"

Mrs Prickleback began hurrying

towards the waterwheel. "The waterwheel has stopped! We must get it turning again. Hurry, everyone!"

The whole hedgehog family scrambled into their little wheels.

"Ready, team?" asked Mr Prickleback.

"Ready!" they cried.

"CURL!" Mr Prickleback shouted.

The Pricklebacks curled up and began rolling. The waterwheel groaned, then it started to turn. Immediately, a trickle of water flowed through the riverbed. Lily and Jess gasped in delight as the trickle grew larger and larger, the water swirling along until Willowtree River was back to normal. All the watching animals cheered as the Pricklebacks came out of the waterwheel and had a family hug.

"I'm c-c-c-cold," said a voice.

The girls turned to see Dusty. She was shivering.

"It looks like you need to get dry again after the water fight," said Jess.

Mrs Prickleback hurried inside and came out with towels for them all. But the dragon was still shivering miserably.

"I-I-I-I'm going to s-s-s-sunbathe," she said, her teeth chattering.

"Dusty can't go back to the Treasure Tree," Goldie whispered in alarm. "What if she turns more fruit into stone?"

"What about Coral Cove," Lily said. "Wouldn't that be a lovely place for Dusty to sunbathe, away from all the animals?"

"We know the perfect place for you to sunbathe, Dusty," Jess told her.

Dusty gave a little smile.

"It's by the river, so you can play in the

water and then get dry again whenever you like." Jess continued.

"We can have another water balloon fight tomorrow!" Emily suggested. "And you can have some of my petals to decorate your scales."

"If you promise not to cause any more trouble," Goldie said firmly.

Dusty's smile turned into a wide grin. She whizzed around them in a happy circle. "I promise! Heeheehee! I'm going to have so much fun!"

They told Dusty where Coral Cove was. She flapped away, giggling.

"I'm glad she's happy," said Lily.

Just then they heard an excited squeal from nearby. All the other creatures were happy too – with the river back to normal, the race could finally begin!

Jess and Lily jumped up and down as all the boats raced down the river as fast as they could. The Pricklebacks had turned the waterwheel so much that the river was gushing and rushing. As they cheered, two boats inched ahead of the others. Everyone shouted loudly for their favourite team.

"Go, go, Greenhops!"

"Faster, faster, Flippershells!"

It was going to be a close finish. The Greenhops' lily pad and the Paddlefoots' canoe were neck and neck as they sped towards the finish line.

Everyone turned to look at the judges excitedly. The swans whispered to each other and everyone in the crowd held their breath.

"Tie!" called Silvia Whitewing. "I declare you both winners!"

With the race over, all the animals spread out blankets and unpacked their picnics. Everyone was excited, and plenty of food-swapping went on. Mrs Twinkletail had brought enough hazelnut chips for half the animals in the forest!

All too soon it was time for the girls to leave. "Thank you!" the animals called as they said goodbye. Emily gave them a special hug before rolling off to play with her brothers.

Goldie took Jess and Lily to the Friendship Tree. She touched the trunk with her paw, and the magical door appeared.

"Thank you for helping us again," she

said. "Grizelda has two more dragons, though. She's bound to think up another wicked plan soon."

"Don't worry, we'll be ready," said Lily.

"Just come and fetch us," Jess added. "We can't wait to see you again, Goldie!"

They hugged their friend goodbye and stepped into the

golden light that shimmered inside the tree. As the glow faded, they found themselves back in Brightley Meadow. As usual, no time at all had passed while they were in Friendship Forest and it was still a misty morning. They had a whole day of fun at Helping Paw to come!

"What a brilliant adventure!" cried Lily as they held hands and ran back towards the wildlife hospital.

They slowed down as they reached the hedge. A little pile of leaves rustled, and out popped the snuffly little hedgehog they'd released earlier. It saw the girls but, to their surprise, it didn't run and hide.

"He must remember that we're friendly," said Jess.

The girls shared a smile. They knew another little hedgehog who was just as clever!

The End

Grizelda's next dragon wants to make the forest inky dark! Find out if Lily, Jess and Goldie can stop him in the next adventure,

Ruby Fuzzybrush's Star Dance

Turn over for a sneak peek . . .

The foxes stepped, dipped, glided and turned around the moonstone, weaving complicated patterns. Each time they swept past each other and their bushy tails touched, the glow from the moonstone grew brighter.

Lily glanced up at the night sky. "Look, Jess!" she whispered. "The stars are coming out."

Jess gazed at the sky. "It's so beautiful!" she cried. "Oh! The brighter the moonstone becomes, the more stars appear."

The girls stared in delight as hundreds

– no, thousands – of stars winked and blinked in the darkness. Soon it was almost as bright as daytime, the forest lit up with sparkling silver starlight.

Suddenly, Rusty cried out, "Look, Mum, Dad! Up there in the sky!"

Read

Ruby Fuzzybrush's Star Dance

to find out what happens next!

Puzzle Fun!

Can you help Emily to find the following words in this magical wordsearch?

U	B	Y	X	Z	A	M	S	A	R
S	W	F	O	R	E	S	T	G	A
E	O	F	C	V	N	E	Y	R	H
F	I	Z	V	M	W	Z	R	I	G
L	U	Q	W	A	W	J	E	Z	W
W	S	S	Y	G	I	U	M	E	I
S	P	E	W	O	U	L	I	L	Y
S	H	C	E	P	A	P	Q	D	P
E	J	E	B	T	I	A	R	A	T
J	R	L	I	L	G	R	Z	M	P

WORDS TO FIND:

Tiara
Forest
Grizelda
Lily
Jess

ANSWERS

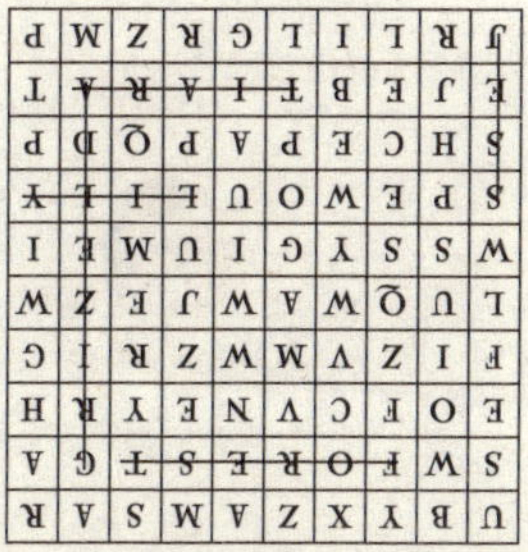

Jess and Lily's Animal Facts

Lily and Jess love lots of different animals – both in Friendship Forest and in the real world.

Here are their top facts about

HEDGEHOGS

like Emily Prickleback

- Hedgehogs are nocturnal animals, which means they only come out at night. If you see one during the day it is probably in trouble and should be taken to a Wildlife Rescue Centre.
- Hedgehogs like to eat beetles, millipedes, worms, slugs and snails.
- Baby hedgehogs are called 'urchins'.
- Lots of people think that hedgehogs like to eat milk and bread, but actually tinned dog or cat food is healthier for them.
- Hedgehogs do not make good pets, but are very good for your garden because they like to eat garden pests like slugs and snails.

Tiggywinkles
Worlds Leading Wildlife Hospital

Lily's parents aren't the only ones who run a wildlife hospital.

Have you heard of Tiggywinkles – the world's busiest wildlife hospital? They take care of over 10,000 poorly animals every year and treat all kinds of wildlife, including hedgehogs, badgers, birds, foxes and deer.

If you are worried about a wild animal, you can have a look at their website for hints and tips about what to do.

www.tiggywinkles.com

Orchard Books supports Tiggywinkles.

Registered Charity No. 286447 Tiggywinkles,
Aston Road, Haddenham, Aylesbury,
Buckinghamshire HP17 8AF UK
Tel: 01844 292292
Email: mail@sttiggywinkles.org.uk